Overcoming The World in

Winning the Game of Life God's Way

STAY STRONG
AND OVERCOME!

- Ben Stevenson

ben stevenson

i

table of Contents

Endorsements

"A great connection between baseball and faith. This would be a great book for athletes of all ages in all sports."
- Ron Polk (former head coach Mississippi State, member of the college baseball Hall of Fame, and author of the" Baseball Playbook" the best selling how-to baseball book of its kind).

"Ben Stevenson is an energetic writer with something to say, and he says it with conviction. His honest, candid approach to life, sports, and values is refreshing and practical. Every person I've ever met could learn something of value from this young man's book."
- Kyle Butt (Apologetics Press).

dedication

I would like to dedicate this book to all the people that helped make it happen. I could not have fulfilled a life long dream of mine without the help of so many people.

To my parents who raised me with the Christian morals and ethics that helped shape my views in this book.

To East Huntsville Church of Christ, Lone Cedar Church of Christ and Florence Boulevard Church of Christ who all played a part in strengthening my faith.

To Paige Runnion who was my first editor.

To Kyle Butt who was my second editor and the one who helped me make this project happen.

To Bruce Jumper for working to help get me endorsements.

To Coach Ron Polk for the endorsement.

To the UNA baseball program and coaches who gave me four great years full of friendships, stories and memories.

To all of my family who believed in me from the very beginning and encouraged me along the way.

To my wife, Linzee, who has been nothing but supportive throughout the entire process of writing this book and getting it published.

All of these people and so many more have helped make this book happen. I am forever indebted to them for their friendship, love and encouragement.

I love you all. God Bless.

Batting Practice

Introduction

Let me start off by telling you a little bit about my-self. I am a nobody, an average Joe. I am not famous, not rich, nor will I probably ever be either of these. I am a simple guy from Harvest, Alabama that is certain of a few things in this world: I love God, I love my family, I love my wife, and I love sports. I am a graduate of the University of North Alabama (UNA) were I studied Secondary Education, and went on to use my degree to become a teacher and coach. I will probably never be a big-name baseball coach, and that is perfectly fine with me. As I said, I am a simple guy and that is prob-ably all I ever will be, and that is good enough.

Now, first let me explain my love for God. This is not a repost and retweet status type of love that I have for the Lord, and it is not a Sunday morning, Sunday night, Wednesday night type of love for the Lord either. This is a 7-day-a-week, 365-day-a-year kind of love I have for the Lord. I work day in and day out to do as I am commanded to do in His word, and I work to set the best example possible to those around me. Now, of course, it goes without saying that I am in no way perfect. I make my fair share of mistakes and have bad days just as everyone else, but I am in the fight to be what I am supposed to be for the Lord. I was raised at the East Huntsville Church of Christ and attended there until I left for college. While attending UNA, I went to a couple of different congregations before finding my home at the Lone Cedar Church of Christ and then eventually going full time with my girlfriend (now wife) and her family to the Florence Boulevard Church of Christ. All three of these churches had a dramatic impact on my life and helped mold me into the Christian man that I am today. East Huntsville was the church that raised me, and that congregation more than prepared me for college and living on my own. Going to worship while in college was a struggle at first as I was coming from a place where everyone had seen me grow up, and I was now going to be going to congregations where no one knew my name. I bounced around a few places before landing at Lone Cedar. I immediately knew that is where I wanted to be while attending church in college. I was immediately welcomed by the entire congregation there, and there were a few people (Eddie Matthews and Colton Scott) that I connected with immediately and am extremely happy to say that we are friends to this day. Once Linzee (my wife) and I started dating I continued to go to Lone Cedar for a while and then realized I wanted to be in worship every Sunday with the woman that I loved and she, of course, was going to continue to go where her family attended. That is when I made the transition to the Florence Boulevard Church of Christ. Again, I was welcomed there immediately, and it would be what I considered my home congregation through the rest of my college years. All of these places and all of the people I met at these places have had a dramatic impact on me, and I am forever grateful for how they have helped me to grow in Christ.

Next, I want to talk about my family and my wife, Linzee. I was lucky enough to be raised in a Christian home with Christian parents. I grew up with three brothers, and all six of us attended worship every time the doors were open simply because my parents would not have it any other way. I mentioned how the church I have attended helped me grow in Christ. Well, my parents are the ones who put the foundation in place. Growing up, I missed ball games (this hurt when I was a kid), social events and many other things because going to church came first in our house. My parents were there to set the example for me and all of my brothers as we grew up, and I know for a fact that the only reason I am the man I am today is because of the parents I was blessed with and the home that I grew up in. Linzee was the person who provided that stronghold for me in college. I met Linzee the spring semester of my sophomore year at UNA, and we have been together ever since. She was always a rock for me to lean on when I had my struggles throughout my college years, and she continues to be that rock for me today. I can know without a doubt that I married a person who has a real goal of getting to heaven and wants to help me achieve that same goal. Yes, the Lord has blessed me in multiple ways when it comes to my family and my wife, and I am forever grateful for all that he has done.

Finally, I need to explain my love for sports. Many people like sports. I LOVE sports. I have been able to take away so much from athletics that I could probably not list it all. I have been affiliated with some sort of sports team since I was five years old, and if it's up to me, I will continue to be until my days are done here on this earth. Every team, every group, every teammate is unique and different, and this is part of what makes sports enjoyable. I simply cannot get enough. I have certain teams that I pull for (Tennessee Volunteers and Atlanta Braves), but I will watch just about every team that plays anything if it is possible. My two main sports are baseball and football. I played both of those all throughout high school before going to UNA, and I coach both of those now. Knowing that I did not have the ability to make it past high school as a player, but unwilling to give up sports, I took a job as a manager for the UNA baseball team that I held for four years. Being around college athletics was an incredible experience, and I consider the players and coaches I worked with in four years at UNA just as much my teammates as I would any other. I knew early on in my life that I wanted to become a coach, and working with UNA's baseball team helped me learn so much in working towards that goal. My 5th year of college (yes, I was on the five-year plan), I did my student internship at Florence High School and was lucky enough to be able to help coach the teams there. This was my first real experience coaching outside of a few summer leagues, and I knew after the first practice that I had made the right career choice. Outside of worship and family, sports is where I feel the most comfortable, and I look forward to hopefully having a long career working with young people in this aspect to help teach them the same life lessons that athletics taught me.

As you can see, the things listed above have all had a dramatic impact on my life up to this point, and I feel there is no doubt that they will continue to influence me in the future. I write this book because the things that make the most sense to me in life are God, family, and athletics, so I wanted to tie all of them together. Most of this book will be the correlation between Christian living and athletics, but know that my family has helped me to understand all of the things that are listed. I feel that man truly can overcome the world just as Christ did (John 16:33), and the lessons that I learned in worship service and in sports have helped and continue to help me realize this even more. This 9-step plan to overcoming the world is no new idea. This has been written in the Lord's word forever; I simply made it into a process. I believe what it says in 1 John 5:4, *"For whatsoever is born of God overcomes the world. And this is the victory that has overcome the world - our faith,"* and I wanted to find a way to help others realize this as well. I have often made mention of the metaphor "The Game of Life" when talking with friends. This is something that I have been able to use as a contrast between what I have learned through athletics and what I have learned in the scripture. In order to win the "Game of Life," we must be willing to win every inning. If we can tackle every inning and give it our best shot, then even when we lose some battles, we can know that we are still not far behind. So my ultimate challenge to you as you read this book is this: Win every inning, win the game of life, and overcome the world. I truly hope this book is beneficial to you and yours as I know writing it has been beneficial to me. Thank you for reading and God Bless.

"Sports remain a great metaphor for life's more difficult lessons. It was through athletics that many of us first came to understand that fear can be tamed; that on a team the whole is more than the sum of its parts; and that the ability to be heroic lies, to a surprising degree, within."
-Susan Casey (author and speaker)

The Game of LIFE

Life is a game,
Full of losses and wins.
The competition starts,
As soon as life begins.

Life is a game,
With emotional highs and lows,
And when the game will end,
No one really knows.

Life is a game,
Where you cannot slack at all,
Because as soon as you begin to,
You will stumble and fall.

Life is a game,
Make it count till the end,
Because how you play the game,
Determines where eternity you'll spend.

-Ben Stevenson

The 1st Inning
Set Goals/Priorities

"If a man wins God's race it doesn't matter where else he loses. If a man loses God's race it doesn't matter where else he wins."
– Steve Lawson (author of 'Men who Win')

In sports, as in life, to obtain something you first have to decide what it is you want to obtain. If a team just went out and played game after game with no real motive, then it would probably be extremely unsuccessful and it would be completely wasting its time. Any team that participates in an athletic event at higher levels of competition wants to win. That is the main motivating factor. The teams that are most successful are the ones who plan out their goals. I remember playing high school baseball, and at the beginning of every year when we had our first team meeting, our coaches would have us write down five personal goals and five team goals for the upcoming season. This was a time where we could really look forward to the season ahead and think about all that we could accomplish together if we were all willing to do our part. Many of us hung those goal sheets in our lockers as a reminder every day when we went to practice. Now, I must admit as a 15 and 16 year old, I probably did not use my goal sheet as a measuring stick as I should have all year. I was pumped about it at first, and I tried to meet my personal goals every day and held myself accountable when I didn't. However, over time I quit looking at that goal sheet and just went about my day-to-day activities doing things as I saw fit. This can be a serious problem in our Christian lives as well.

When we first become new Christians or after some big event like a revival, lectureship, or church camp, we get pumped up about living the right Christian life and hold ourselves accountable for the things that we do and do not do day to day. However, over time, when we are back around the world every day, we lose our luster somewhat and fall right back to doing the same old things the way we see fit. Philippians 3:14 says, *"I press toward the goal for the prize of the upward call of God in Christ Jesus."* This should be our thought every single day when we wake up. We should want to start every day pressing toward the mark for the prize of the high calling. If we set out to make that our number one goal each day then there is no doubt that we will be living up to goals that we originally set for ourselves when we first became Christians.

Daily reminders are something that can truly drive people to do what they need to do so that they can go where they want and need to go. This can be done in a number of different ways from notes on the bathroom mirror to pictures on the wall, but I do strongly suggest that you find some way to remind yourself daily of the ultimate goal of living a life for Christ and setting an example to all of those around you. Within the last year, I posted a sign in my room across from my bed that read "According to Whose Standard." This was my daily reminder to make sure I was living my life according to God's standard. It is easy sometimes to justify sin and to have the "everyone else is doing it" kind of mind-set. We have to be set apart from the rest of the world according to Romans 12:2, *"And do not be conformed to this world, but be transformed by the renewing of your mind, that you may prove what is that good and acceptable and perfect will of God,"* and the only way to do that is to live according to His standard. This is my daily goal as I start every day, and I honestly can say that this reminder I see every morning to keep my goal has helped me grow closer to God in my daily walk. So, I strongly challenge you to write down your goals. Have them listed in a diary or on a scratch sheet of paper. Where they are does not matter as much as your willingness to look at them as a reminder of what you are striving for in this sinful world in which we live and how your daily goals can help you reach that ultimate goal of getting to Heaven.

Now let's talk about the ever-important topic of priorities. By now, hopefully, you have listed your goals and have found a way to remind yourself of these daily goals so that you will achieve them. The next big step is prioritizing your life so that your goals can be achieved. I mentioned in the Preface of this book how

I was lucky enough to grow up in a Christian home with Christian parents who made it a point to put God first in both their lives and in the lives of their children. This meant that at times I had to miss out on doing the things that all kids love to do, like play little league. I loved playing little league baseball at the local park and recreation. It was fun, all my friends played, and ever since I was little, I always loved the idea of competition (this makes since knowing that I grew up with 3 brothers).

Unfortunately, my park and rec seemed to have a ritual, perhaps just to torture me, where it seemed that every rained out game was made up on Wednesday night. Of course, in my house Wednesday night was church night, and I was not going to be with the rest of my team playing in that game. I would pout and complain over and over again to my mom (notice I just mentioned mom; you did not pout and complain to my father) about how it wouldn't hurt to just miss one service and I was just going to be thinking about the game anyway so there was no point in me going to church at all. She was not having it. I was going to be in church on Wednesday night, and if maybe for some reason the game went late and it was still going on after church I could catch the very end of it. What I did not realize then was that my missing that game was not about God sending me to hell for missing one Wednesday night service, and it was not about my parents trying to make me miserable. It was about showing me through their actions that baseball and trivial things of this earth were not and are not more important than worship services.

It was not until I got older into my high school years that I really got this for the first time. I remember perfectly one Wednesday night we had a make-up game against Bob Jones (my school's biggest rival), and I would be able to stay for game one, but game two started around 7:00, and that is when church started. I knew whenever we played double headers I usually got to play at least one of the games, but it was usually the second one. I was called on to pinch hit in the last inning of game one. I grounded out to the first baseman, and that would be all of the baseball I played that night. I got in the car with Mom, and I was a bit upset. I knew I would probably start game two, and it was Bob Jones for crying out loud. This was a game that I wanted to play in, and I wanted to win. I made a quick comment about how I wanted to stay and play game two. Mom stopped the car and turned around quickly and said, "You're old enough to make that decision on your own. If you want to stay, get out of the car." I quickly said I did not, and we went on to church in silence. I had mainly said no because I knew that (1) it would make Mom mad if I stayed and (2) I knew deep down that it was the right thing to do. I thought about it as we drove to church silently, and it would have gone against everything I stood for if my friends saw me come back into the dugout and miss church service. The Stevenson's did not miss church service and if I decided I wanted to by choice, then what example would that have set to all of my friends? This was my first real lesson in prioritizing my life in order to reach my goals. From there on out, I remember I missed numerous Wednesday night baseball games without hesitation or second thought. That was who I was going to be. God was going to be more important than baseball - end of story.

I believe this is another area where we sometimes make mistakes as Christians. We make our goals and may even remind ourselves of these goals, but we do not prioritize our lives in a way that allows us to reach those goals. This is a key step to winning inning 1. We can have a laundry list full of goals and tell everyone what our goals are, but it is only when we get our priorities straight that we will really begin to see our goals achieved. Matthew 6: 19-21 says, *"Do not lay up for yourselves treasure on earth, where moth and rust destroy and where thieves break in and steal; but lay up for yourselves treasures in heaven, where neither moth nor rust destroys and where thieves do not break in and steal. For where your treasure is, there your heart will be also."* This scripture states it as clearly as it can be stated. Our treasures, our goals, our priorities have to be set in place with heavenly ambitions. I love all sports, but more than all, I love the game of baseball. It is a release for me from all the stresses that the world can sometimes bring. However, if baseball is my number one priority in life, I am going to have one long, rough road ahead, maybe not here on this earth but, even worse, for all eternity. We read in Mark 10: 17-22 where Jesus was talking to the rich young ruler. This rich man had asked Jesus what he needed to do to inherit eternal life. Christ answered him, "You know the commandments: 'Do not commit adultery,' 'Do not murder,' 'Do not steal,' 'Do not bear false witness,' 'Do not defraud,' 'Honor your father and your mother." Of course, the rich young ruler responded, "Teacher, all these have I have kept from my youth." It was then that Jesus gave the rich young ruler the answer that he did not want to hear more than anything in the world. "One thing you lack: Go your way, sell whatever you have and give to the poor, and you will have treasure in heaven; and come, take up the cross, and follow Me." We read in verse 22 that the rich young ruler "went away sorrowful, for he had great possessions." One small thing kept this man from inheriting the eternal life that he sought after at the beginning of the story. The love of an earthly thing kept him from what he knew was right. It is sad to see in our society today so many people who know to do right, but the love of one earthly thing keeps them from being the Christian they need to be. We read in James 2: 10, *"For whoever shall keep the whole law, and yet stumble in one point, he is guilty of all."* We have to be willing to be 100% Christian all of the time, and that starts with setting the right goals and then setting our priorities in a way that allows us to meet those goals. We have to be willing to fully buy in to the Christian lifestyle and realize that the juice is definitely worth the squeeze.

As Christians, I think it is important to realize that we all should have the exact same goals:

- Get to heaven.
- Take as many people with us along the way.

These goals are both selfish and evangelistic. When it comes to the sake of your soul for all eternity, there is nothing in the world wrong with being selfish. Rule number one is to take care of number one because your soul should mean the most to you, and it is going to be pretty hard to convert somebody if you are not where you need to be yourself. We are a consistent work in progress and can always and should always take the opportunity to learn more. That being said, those of us who are well enough along in our Christian lives need to be spreading the good news of the gospel as we are commanded to in Matthew 28:19-20.

The goal here in this 9 inning process is to win every inning. If you do not win inning number one, you will have to play catch up for the next few innings, and your opponent, Satan, is not going to take it easy on you. In your struggle to overcome the world, your opponent wants to see you fail more than ever, and he is willing to do whatever necessary to make sure that happens. So, lessons to take from inning number 1:

Set goals, write down these goals so that you can be reminded of what you are working to accomplish, and prioritize your life so that you put yourself in a position to achieve your goals. If you can do that, it's 1-0 you after inning number one.

> *"If you don't make a total commitment to what-ever you're doing, then you start looking to bail out the first time the boat starts leaking. It's tough enough getting that boat to shore with everybody rowing, let alone when a guy stands up and starts putting on his life jacket."*
>
> *-Lou Holtz*

The 2nd Inning

Practice/Study

"Failing to prepare is preparing for failure."
– John Wooden

Let's be honest - no one really ever likes to practice. You may like it for a day or two, but then it gets long and tiresome. I can remember playing football in high school, and I don't know that I can ever remember being excited about practice. Maybe the first day of spring training, but that would be about it. The last thing I wanted to do after I had been in school all day was go put on 50 pounds worth of pads in the blazing Alabama sun and let a free safety and linebacker tee off on me for 3 hours. I got my bell rung more than once in my tenure playing football, but looking back on it, without the agony of practice, I would have never been able to enjoy Friday night games. Now this, on the other hand, I looked forward to all day, every Friday. Baseball was my favorite sport growing up, but it is hard to describe the feeling of a Friday night football game unless you just experience it yourself, especially in the south. I loved the anticipation all day, wearing my jersey to school, pep rallies, and then nothing beat when those lights cut on a few hours before the game and we went out for pregame warm-ups. These Friday nights are something that I will remember for the rest of my life. However, these great memories could never have happened without the Monday through Thursday practice that I dreaded. It is all about the process. As an athlete you have to be willing to go to work to get better every day or you will simply get left behind. The old saying, "Hard work beats talent when talent doesn't work hard" could never be more true in both athletics and in life. Those who are simply content with the talents they have been given and care nothing about expanding those talents will soon be nothing more than average. I once heard a coach say, "The man on top of the mountain didn't fall there." What a concept. In order to get to the top of your game, you have to be willing to buy in to the process and the steps necessary to get to the top of the mountain.

Looking back on my college years at UNA, I loved being the baseball manager. I was able to work on the front lines with a top NCAA Division II collegiate baseball team, and I was able to gain so much experience from that. I was in a unique situation where I was the players' age and in close with them, but I was also around the coaches much more and heard everything they had to say. I got to hear why the players hated certain things that we did, and I got to hear the coaches explain why we did those very same things. It was amazing to me that every year the most successful players we had on our team were the ones that were willing to put in the extra work. We practiced or played

6 days a week, and when we practiced, it was all out, all the time. When practice was over, many of the players gladly went home to relax, but others stayed behind to get in some extra ground balls or some extra cuts in the cage. It was no coincidence that these players were usually the most successful in games. This got me to thinking about my baseball playing days in high school. Let me start by making this very clear: I was extremely average. Never a great ball player but not terrible either. I went to a big 6A school, and we had a good number of players try out for the team every year, so the fact that I made the squad for 4 years is something to be proud of. However, at times I feel that I was content with just that. Now, I would never have admitted that back then, and if you would have accused me of this, I would have probably blown up and called you a liar. But as I look back, I think I was too content with being on the team. I went to practice every day, and at the end of practice, I went home. I knew my skill set, and I knew that the only way to get better was to work harder than everybody else, but I didn't. Why? Probably because it would have consisted of more work than I wanted to put in, and it would have taken away from my "me" time. How crazy is that, right? It is the guys who are willing to work all the time that will be the most successful. Those who just want to get off the bus and play will never be anything more than extremely average. This could never be more true when applied to our Christian lives. We can't be Sunday morning, Sunday night, Wednesday night, "get off the

bus and play" type of Christians. If the only time we pick up our Bibles is when the preacher tells us to turn to a particular scripture or when we are asked to read aloud in Bible class, then we have a serious problem! We read in 2 Timothy 2:15, *"Study to show thyself approved unto God, a workman that needeth not to be ashamed, rightly dividing the word of truth."* Things cannot get any clearer than this verse when it comes to how we are to study the word of God. The only way to continue to grow in Christ is to study His word in order to learn. I know many Christians who leave their Bible in their car so that it will be with them whenever they get out to go in to the church building. I even know some people who leave their Bible on the pew so that it is there waiting for them when they get to worship services. I'm sure you know certain people like this as well and who knows - you may even be one of them. If this applies to you, I beg and plead with you to start studying your Bible. It is not going to read itself, and you are not going to learn God's word simply through osmosis. When it comes to eternal life and your salvation, do you really just want to be extremely average? Are you content with making the team and not willing to work in order to get better? We have to study and we have to be willing to learn. There is no way we will win another inning if we refuse to win this one.

Sam Ewing was an outfielder in the majors during the 1970's. He graduated from the University of Tennessee and was drafted by the Chicago White Sox in

1973. Sam had a career average of .255 with 6 home runs and 47 runs batted in when his career ended with the Toronto Blue Jays in 1978. You may be thinking, "These are not impressive statistics," and you would be correct; however, it was not for lack of effort. One thing Sam was willing to do was work hard. He is quoted as saying, "Hard work spotlights the character of people; some turn up their sleeves, some turn up their noses, and some don't turn up at all." This is the big challenge that we all need to take on as a Christian people. When it comes to studying God's word, are we going to turn up our sleeves and get after it? Are we going to turn up our noses and think, "I will do that on Sunday, but I have better things to do now"? Or are we going to not turn up at all and say, "I don't need to study; I already know all I need to know"? I hope for your sake that you are going to choose option number one.

Always remember that hard work costs you nothing, but not working hard can cost you everything. As Christians, we should be excited to learn more about God's word. If we are serious about meeting the goals that we set in inning one, then we must be willing to practice and put in the time and effort to achieve these goals. You will notice throughout this book that you really can't have one inning without the other. That is what makes this game complete. We have to win every inning because it is impossible to win the others if we don't. Practice and study is something that often goes overlooked in today's day and age. Many want to be a get-off-the-bus-and-play Christian and hope that will be enough. I am here to tell you that it is not. Not because I say so but because that is what our heavenly Father says. So, I challenge you in this inning to go out and get better. Don't be content with being extremely average, and don't be content with just being on the team. Let's go get better every day and continue to work to overcome the world.

> *"We are what we do repeatedly.   Excellence, then, is not an act, but a habit."*
>
> *-Aristotle*

The 3rd Inning

Surround Yourself With Winners

"The winners in life think constantly in terms of I can, I will, and I am. Losers, on the other hand, concentrate their waking thoughts on what they should have or would have done, or what they can't do."
-Dennis Waitley (famous author and keynote speaker)

The concept to inning number three is nothing new at all. It is a tale as old as time some might say. Peer pressure has been and always will be the greatest motivator. It was when I was 16 years old, still is now that I am 23 years old, and I would dare to say that it will continue to be for the rest of my life. Sadly enough, we depend way too much on what we get from people and not nearly enough on what we get from God. Why is this? It is probably due largely in part to the fact that we are a people of quick results. We want what we want and we want it now! I have seen this even more so over the past year. I have recently become certified to be a personal trainer. I have always enjoyed working out and staying fit, and I wanted to help other people reach their goals. Now, let me first say that the people I train (at least as of now) are extremely hard workers. They really push themselves (which we will talk about in the later innings), and I feel they have seen results.

However, the more I am up at the gym, the more I see people expecting that magic doorway to help them lose their weight. They expect to walk in the gym doors and suddenly they have dropped 5 pounds. This is the way we sometimes think about everything in life. We want results now, and we want gratitude now, and man can give us that, but if we will just hold off and wait, then our reward will be beyond compare. Nonetheless, no matter how you slice it, we, as people, will always be concerned about what others think about us, and therefore, we are at times willing to conform to what people want us to be instead of being who we know we should. You may wonder the best way to combat that. Simple - surround yourself with winners. This is a basic concept that has been a well-known fact in sports since well before my time. Winners breed success, and the more they stick together, the more successful they will be.

I can remember during my second year of working with the UNA baseball team, we had one of, if not the, most talented teams we had in all my four years working with the program. I was really excited for the year to start, and I liked the team and felt good about our chances of going far. Unfortunately, I could never have been more wrong. There were a few players that seemed to have the team and winning as the last thing on their minds. The season started and other things become more important than helping the team win. These "cancers" as I call them, can destroy team chemistry and turn a great team into an average team. We had some leaders on the team that tried to turn things around, but it just was not going to happen. We finished the year without a conference tournament bid, and what looked like it could be a great season turned in to something much different. On the flip side of that, my fourth and final year working with the baseball team, we had a team that was absolutely inseparable. If you have ever been around college athletics, you know that, as players on a team, you see each other more than you do anyone else in the world. Your family, girlfriend, it doesn't matter. They better get used to not seeing much of you during the season. At times, this causes players to want to get away from each other a little bit when they are not at practice, on the road, or at a game. This could not be further from the truth with the 2012 UNA Lion baseball team. On Friday night of every home weekend, the guys all went out to see a movie together. They constantly were at one another's houses or apartments, and I honestly feel that if they could have found a 30-bedroom house, they would have gladly all lived there together. Now, I knew we had a pretty good team after fall practice was over, but I had given up on getting excited about what could be because of let downs in the past. So, I went into the season with the thought that yeah, we could be good, but we will see. All in all, that story ends with us getting a NCAA Regional bid and being two wins away from a trip to the Division II World Series. I don't want to make it sound like the only reason we were good was because of our team chemistry because that is not true. We had players step up when we needed them to, and the team was very talented. However, I do feel that the fact that everyone on that team had the same goal of a championship in mind helped drive us to be as good as we were. See, when you have a group of people driving and fighting for the same thing, you are ten times more likely to see that goal achieved because those people standing beside you are going to make sure that you don't let up. That is the power of being surrounded by winners.

Our Christian lives really are no different when it comes to the people with whom you surround yourself. While at UNA, I, along with two friends (Colton Scott and Tyler Alexander), decided to start up a religious-type blog. We felt that we had some good thoughts that we wanted to share with people, and if nothing else, hopefully it could touch someone who didn't really know what being a Christian was all about and we could study with them. This was a small-scale type of blog that we eventually turned into a website: *www.thestand613.webs.com.* On the home page of this site, we listed our goals as a group and they go as follows:

• 1: Get to Heaven
• 2: Take as many people with us as we can along the way.

This is a simple concept but powerful nonetheless. You can replace the word winners in this chapter with Christians and you will have found the people with whom you need to surround yourself. Now, I am not talking about those Sunday morning and Sunday night only "Christians." I'm talking about people who are willing to live it all the time. You may be asking yourself, "How can I determine the difference between the real Christians and the 'wolves in sheep's clothing' that are referred to in Matthews 7:15?" (*"Beware of false prophets, who come to you in sheep's clothing, but inwardly they are ravenous wolves."*) See, the idea behind surrounding yourself with Christians is finding people who are willing to win innings 1 and 2. If you can find those people that set their goals and priorities that line up with what your goals and priorities are, and if you can find people who are willing to practice and study to obtain those goals, then you have found some company that you need to keep. We read in 2 Corinthians 6:14, *"Do not be unequally yoked together with unbelievers. For what fellowship has righteousness with lawlessness? And what communion has light with darkness."* Paul lays it out clearly here in his second letter to the Corinthians that we are not we be yoked together or set together with the unbelievers because the righteous and the wicked have nothing in common. Why would I be willing to risk my own salvation just to be friends with a person who has no goals or aspirations of becoming a resident of heaven? First Corinthians 15:33 says, *"Do not be deceived: evil company corrupts good habits."* We all know that old saying, if you lie with the dogs, you are going to get fleas. If we constantly put ourselves together with non-Christians, then we run the risk of losing our own salvation. Now, that being said, do not misunderstand me and think I am saying never talk to or associate with a non-Christian. Jesus did such daily as he worked as a soul winner for His heavenly Father. However, He did not keep company with these people nor was He willing to let their thoughts corrupt His thoughts. We need to be willing to talk to and work with non-Christians as we want to spread the good news of the Gospel, but before we do so, we must have won inning 2 and done our practice and study. (Notice how all these innings build on one another. You must win one in order to win the next.)

There is no greater example of this than Jesus Christ. This is the son of God, and He was faced with temptation just as we are every day, but He was able to fight off that temptation even when Satan offered Him all the kingdoms of the world (Matthew 4: 8-10). Jesus knew that the reward and gratitude He would receive from man would not be near as sweet as the ultimate reward He would receive in heaven. I have no doubt that what helped to keep Jesus strong while here on this earth was that He surrounded Himself with winners. He went out and found twelve apostles who, while still having much to learn, had the same goals as He did. One may say, well what about Judas? He deceived Jesus and then hung himself, so how did he have the same goals as Christ did?

Remember that "cancer" we talked about earlier in the chapter? Judas was exactly that. In an extremely short time, Judas betrayed Jesus, Peter denied Jesus three times, Jesus was hung on the cross, Judas hanged himself and the apostles went their separate ways. However, because Christ had been a mentor leader to His apostles, they were not down and out once He was gone. They all came back when Jesus rose from the dead and Peter, that guy who denied Christ three times, preached the first sermon on the day the church was founded (Day of Pentecost: Acts 2). Christ surrounded Himself with winners, and because of that, not only do I feel they helped to keep Him strong while He was here on this earth but, He was able to teach them things that allowed them to be leaders of the church when He was gone. What a concept!

I know at times it can be difficult to exclude yourself from things on this earth that a Christian really should not be doing. It is hard to disassociate yourself from people who you have always known and thought are good people but do not have the same type of spiritual goals that you have. As I mentioned at the beginning of the chapter, peer pressure is the biggest motivator, and at some point, it gets to all of us. But we read in Mark 9:43-48, *"If your hand causes you to sin, cut it off. It is better for you to enter into life maimed, rather than having two hands, to go to hell, into the fire that shall never be quenched - 'where their worm does not die, and the fire is not quenched.' And if your foot causes you to sin, cut it off. It is better for you to enter life lame, rather than having two feet, to be cast into hell, into the fire that shall never be quenched – 'where their worm does not die, and the fire is not quenched.' And if you eye causes you to sin, pluck it out. It is better for you to enter the kingdom of God with one eye, rather than having two eyes, to be cast into hell fire – 'where their worm does not die, and the fire is not quenched."* Now, if Jesus is saying here that we should "Pluck out our own eye" if it keeps us from heaven, then I think it is safe to say that we should remove those people in our lives who will keep us from heaven. I'm not saying never speak to them again, but realize that those are not the people and those are not the things with which you as a Christian want to be associated.

So, what can we take from the 3rd inning? We should want to surround ourselves with winners - people who are working and striving to win the game of life. We should be with the kind of people who set the same goals as we did in the 1st inning and people who will practice and study to see those goals achieved as mentioned in the 2nd inning. If we refuse to do this, it will be impossible to win any innings after this one. We can't be who we need to be and go where we need to go if we are constantly being held back. Surround yourself with winners. Work together toward common goals, and work together to bring others over to the winning team: God's team.

> *"Bear Bryant's Three Rules for Coaching: 1: Surround yourself with people who can't live without football. 2: Recognize winners. They come in all forms. 3: Have a plan for everything."*

The 4th Inning

Know Your Role

"The measure of who we are is what we do with what we have."
-Vince Lombardi

This is something that I feel is lost on many of the youth in athletics today. There are so many kids who want to be the starting quarterback or running back but are built to be an offensive lineman. Not everyone can play the "star" positions, but that does not mean that their job is any less important. Have you ever thought about how much a quarterback or running back would get pounded without someone to block for them? The career span for NFL QB's and RB's would be a year or two at most! Every job is important, even if you don't get your name in the paper. Look at baseball for example. In the "steroid era" that I saw in my lifetime, it suddenly became all about the long ball. Everyone wanted to hit home runs, and this trickled down to little league parks where kids felt like they had to swing under the ball to hit it up in the air and over the fence. However, how many solo home runs win ball games? Not many. Somebody has to be on base so that home runs can really do some damage. That is where the contact hitters come in to play. Their hits may not be on the ESPN Sports Center Top 10, but they are just as important.

I have seen this idea of knowing your role play out in real life. First off, I have firsthand experience with this as a baseball player in high school. I may have mentioned in the previous chapters that I was an extremely average baseball player. Not great but not terrible either. My main job every game was to be the courtesy runner for our catcher.In high school baseball, there can be a courtesy runner for the catcher and pitcher in the game. Whenever they get on base, a player off the bench can come in and run for them so that they will be in the dugout when the last out is made and can get warmed up between innings as quickly as possible. The courtesy runner does nothing more than wait for the pitcher or catcher to get on base (I always ran for our catcher), and then the coach calls time and he runs out to take his position at the base. Now, this is not an ideal position for anyone to play. Your playing time is completely dependent upon another player, and when you steal a base or score a run, often times it still goes on that other player's stats. Yet, this is a position that still needs to be filled to help the team win games. If I understood anything while playing high school sports, I understood that I wanted to do whatever I needed to do to help my team win and if that meant I was the courtesy runner for our catcher every game then so be it. That is exactly what I was going to do. The second example of a "know your role" situation came during my work with the baseball team at UNA. It was my senior year, and I have already mentioned in previous chapters the amount of success we were able to have that year. This was due in large part to 1.) The team chemistry and 2.) Everybody knowing their role. The most specific example of this came from a senior named Nick McGregor. Nick had come to UNA the year before from a junior college in Mississippi. He was a shortstop, and he definitely had some ability. He was tall and had good range to be able to go deep into the hole to make plays. Nick, or "Greg" as we all called him, had a decent junior season as a Lion, but the coaching staff knew that he was capable of more, and I think that Greg knew it as well. During the off season headed into Greg's senior year, we signed a young shortstop by the name of Josh Carpenter. He was not as tall as Nick, but he had some good range and had a cannon of an arm. When the spring came around and we prepared for our first game, Greg was still our starting shortstop, but Josh, or "Carp," (yes, everyone has a nickname) had not been redshirted, and he still was in the mix to get some playing time. Well, Greg did not at all start the season the way he or the coaching staff had hoped, and in a midweek game at Christian Brothers University, Carp got his first start. I don't remember his exact stats (I'm not superhuman, people), but I know Carp had a great game. I really did not think much of it until I saw the line-up posted for game 1 that Saturday, and Carp's name was penciled in as the starting shortstop. Of course, Greg was not thrilled (who would be), but he and Carp had developed a good friendship, and he hoped all the best for him. Well, Carp did extremely well (eventually becoming the conference freshman of the year), and it looked like Greg was destined for the bench and a few pinch hitting roles for the rest of the season. However, Greg continued to show up every day and work hard. It would have been easy for him to cash it in and realize he was a senior and this would be it for him, but he did exactly the opposite. And let's just say it paid off twofold. Later in the season when we had some trouble finding outfielders to fit certain roles, the coaches came to Greg and asked if he would be willing to give the outfield a shot. Wanting to do whatever was necessary to help the team win, he was more than willing to take on the challenge and began practicing in the outfield that afternoon. To make a long story short, Greg eventually became our starting right fielder and played a pivotal role in the overall success that we had as a team that year. This is a perfect example of how knowing your role can pay dividends for you in the future. Greg understood the move that the coaches had made, but he was not satisfied with simply sitting on the bench and watching every game, so he continued to work hard. I will remember Greg as our starting right fielder and not as a shortstop that was benched.

This "know your role" concept has a direct effect on us as Christians in the Lord's church. We all have some form of ability, no matter what that may be. Some people are extremely gifted in speaking, some in singing, some in reading scripture, prayer, teaching classes, visiting the sick, etc. There is a laundry list of work that needs to be done in the Lord's church, and we all must be willing to do our part to help out. Romans 12:4-7 says, *"For as we have many members in one body, but all the members do not have the same function, so we being many, are one body in Christ, and individually members of one another. Having then gifts differing according to the grace that is given to us, let us use them: if prophecy let us prophesy in proportion to our faith; or ministry let us use it in our ministering; he who teaches, in teaching…"* Here we are given the example of how, just as all the body parts make up the one body, we, as different members, make up the Lord's church. Just as each body part has a different function, so do we as members in the church. We must know our role and be willing and ready to do whatever necessary to help the church grow and succeed as we work to bring others to know the word of God. A role as simple as a front door greeter plays an important role in the reaching out of the church. And if you are not happy with your role and you feel you have the talents and ability to do more, don't be satisfied with where you are. It is all about knowing your role, but it is also about knowing your talents and what role best suits your talents. I'm sure many of us have heard the story about the one talent man in Matthew 25. In verse 15-18, we read, *"And to one he gave five talents, to another two, and to another one, to each according to his own ability; and immediately he went on a journey then he who had received the five talents went and traded with them, and made another five talents. And likewise he who had received two gained two more also. But he who had received one went and dug in the ground, and hid his lord's money."* The parable goes on to call the one talent man a wicked a slothful servant as he did not use his talent wisely, as had the others, out of fear. We cannot be this way as Christians. If you think you have a talent or a particular skill set that can benefit the Lord's work then share it with others. Do not be scared and think others will think it is stupid or not useful. We must be willing to utilize all the tools and abilities that the good Lord has given us, and then we must find our role and help the church grow.

Inning 4 is, just as the others, a very simple concept. We must know our role and how we fit into the church. We must be willing and able to recognize our talents and use them to help the church in whatever way possible. This can not only help us become stronger Christians, but it can help to bring others to know Christ as well. Figure out your talent, use your talent, know your role, and help the church grow.

> *"I was a college coach for thirty –three years, and I never believed a boy was too small. If he could play I'd find a spot for him. You can't have too many good players. Good players win you games. Not big players."*
>
> *-Lynn "Pappy" Swann*

Push Yourself

"There is no substitute for hard work and effort beyond the call or mere duty. That is what strengthens the soul and ennobles one's character." -Walter Camp

The 5th inning is all about self-motivation. You may have done well so far to win innings 1-4, but without the ability to self-motivate, your game will slowly begin to decline from here on out. The first four innings simply prepared us for what was to come in the last five innings. We have set our goals and priorities, practiced and studied to prepare ourselves to reach those goals, surrounded ourselves with winners to help us reach those goals, and understood our role and talents that make us who we are in the game of life. Now comes what some would consider the hard part as we have to put all the things we have learned to good use and push ourselves to do more and to learn more. This, of course, all comes down to our self-motivation (get used to me saying that a lot during this inning).

The idea of pushing yourself has been a part of sports since the beginning of time. In order for all the parts of a team to work correctly, each person has to have his/her own self-motivation to help that team be successful. I talked back in the 1st inning about how we were to set goals, and I touched on how when I played baseball in high school, we were to set team goals and individual goals. Little did we know that these were really one in the same. We set teams goals such as win x number of games, make the playoffs, win a state championship, etc. What we did not realize was that when we wrote down our individual goals, we were writing down what we were going to do to make those team goals happen. If I want to get 200 swings in the cages per day, make no errors in practice, etc., then what I am really doing is pushing myself to improve my game. If all the players on a team are willing to push themselves through self-motivation to improve their game, the team will undoubtedly become a better ball club. We must be willing to push ourselves.

Within the past year or two, I have taken up running as a means to stay physically fit. I no longer play any sports, but I am not the kind of person that can enjoy retirement (that's what I call it) and just sit on the couch and do nothing. So about two years ago, I had a friend come to me and ask me to participate in a 5K race with him. I had always liked running for the most part, so I agreed. I began to train for this race, and I was actually excited about saying I competed in a 5K, and I was excited to see how well I would do. However, it did not take long for this excitement to die off, and I found every excuse in the book not to go run. I put it off and put it off. Finally, race day was a week away, and it had been too long since I had been out for a good run.

Yet, I did agree to the race, so I was not going to back out now. Race day came, and I felt okay about how I would do. I knew I hadn't run in a while, but I used to run a decent amount, and I figured "There is no way I can drop off that quickly." I was wrong. Really, really wrong. The race started, and I took off with a goal in mind to start out front and stay out front (I missed the pace yourself memo). I was in the top 10 for about half a mile, and then I slowly started to fall to the middle of the pack. At the 2 mile marker, I thought I was near death, and it felt like I was wearing concrete blocks for shoes. Finally, by the 2½ mile mark, I had to stop and walk. This tore me up because I had always prided myself on being able to run all the way through things and finish, but there was just no way that was going to happen. I picked it back up and finally crossed the finish line (3.1 miles) at a time of 27:09 (yes, I remember the exact time). I was 21 when I ran that first race, and I am extremely embarrassed to say that a 61-year-old man finished with a time of 27:18 just 9 second behind me! As I walked around after the race trying to keep from losing last night's dinner, I thought to myself, "NEVER AGAIN!" I knew that my racing days were over, and I was just not cut out for this kind of sport. However, about a month later, I got a call from a friend whose school was hosting a 5K to raise money, and since he knew I had done one before, he asked if I would run it with him. Against my better judgment, I agreed, and I knew that this time I was going to have to stay motivated to train. I stuck with my training and finished a whole 2 minutes faster than my first race and felt I still had more in the tank when it was over. From then on, I was hooked. I signed up for multiple 5K's and even some 10K's, always working to do better than I had done before. My fastest 5K time to this day is a 23:13, not great but much improved on that 27:09 I originally ran. Running is a sport that is all self-motivating. If you are not willing to push yourself to train and push yourself during a race, then you might as well hang it up and find something else do to because you are going to see zero success. YOU HAVE TO PUSH YOURSELF!

I was surfing the web one day and came across a sports blog that really caught my attention. It was by a college basketball coach (at this point I don't remember which coach because I started following so many over the years), and there was some really great insight on the blog. There were a few things from this blog that I wrote down to take with me as I became a coach, and I wanted to share one of them with you:

What can you learn from watching players run sprints?
- •1. Are they simply trying to not be last?
- •2. Are they just trying to finish?
- •3. Are they mad because of having to run sprints?
- •4. Are they trying to win every single sprint?

This is something that really stood out to me because one thing I prided myself on while playing high school sports was trying to win every single sprint. I was by no means the most athletic kid on the team, and I was not even close to the fastest. Rarely did I ever actually win every single sprint or any for that matter, but it would not be for lack of effort. Quite possibly the greatest compliment I ever received during my high school athletics days was from an assistant football coach during summer workouts. We had already lifted weights and had been running for a while, and we were finishing the morning (yes, these things started at 7:00 a.m. during the summer) off with 100-yard sprints. After we had run the first two and were standing on the starting line huffing and puffing, one of the coaches said aloud, "I'll tell ya this about Stevenson - He may not win every sprint, but he is going to run that last one as hard as he ran the first one." I must admit I swelled up with a bit of pride in that moment just as anybody would when they feel good that their hard work is noticed. Are you running God's race simply because you have to? Are you just trying not to finish last? Are you complaining about the "fun" things you have had to miss out on in life? Or are you pushing yourself to win the race? *"Do you not know that those who run in a race all run, but one receives the prize? Run in such a way that you may obtain it."* 1 Corinthians 9:24.

We read in 1 Corinthians 15:58, *"Therefore, my beloved brethren, be steadfast, immovable, always abounding in the work of the Lord, knowing that your labor is not in vain in the Lord."* We must be willing to push ourselves in our daily walk with Christ knowing that the work we do is never done in vain, and the finish line is always near. We do not know when our life here on this earth will end; and therefore, we must never let up. Now, life is a marathon, not a sprint, but pacing oneself at the back of the pack never got anyone anywhere but a last place finish. We must always be abounding in the work of the Lord and pushing ourselves to do bigger and better things in His service. When we let up and decide that we are finished running, we have turned our back on all the hard work and preparation we have put in and most importantly, turned our back on the Lord. Luke 9:62 says, *"But Jesus said to him, 'No one, having put his hand to the plow, and looking back, is fit for the kingdom of God."* We must not be a people that work for a while and then cash it in and say that we are finished working for now and will pick it up again another time. What happens if that time never comes? What if life as we know it is cut short and we never have an opportunity to get back in the race? We have given up the greatest reward of all simply because we lost our self-motivation. That being said, we, as Christians, have a responsibility to help motivate others around us. We are all in this race together, and as mentioned in the previous innings, we should want to take others to heaven with us. We have to push ourselves, but we must also be willing to push others as we continue in this race of life. As we run, let's encourage those around us. Let's help them find that extra pep in their step to get them where they need to be. If we see a brother or sister falling behind and contemplating dropping out of the race, we need to be willing to push them to stick with it and finish. Granted, we can't make someone run who chooses not to, but we can do all we can to get them back in the race.

So what can we take way from the 5th inning? Self-motivation is the only motivation that is going to get us where we want to be. We can hear all the words of encouragement we want, but until we are willing to decide within ourselves that we are in a race worth running and that not finishing is not an option, then we will never be successful. We can win innings 1-4, but if we have no self-motivation, no "want-to", and no ability to push ourselves when the going gets tough, then we will bow out of the game early. "So run, that ye may obtain" and know that we are in a race worth running. A race that, when finished, has the ultimate reward.

> *"You can motivate by fear, and you can motivate by reward. But both those methods are only temporary. The only lasting thing is self-motivation."*
>
> *-Homer Rice*

The 6th Inning

Stay Humble

"Discipline and diligence are up there on the list, but one of the most important qualities of many really successful people is humility. If you have a degree of humility about you, you have the ability to take advice, to be coachable, teachable. A humble person never stops learning." - Todd Blackledge

There is a reason that the principle found in the 6th inning follows those found in both innings 4 and 5. To know your role is to remain humble in all the things you do. Those who truly know their role are those who are humble. The problem lies when we push ourselves to do great things, and at times, we feel that we deserve all the credit for what we have done. We want to walk around town and tell everyone what we did and what we accomplished instead of simply letting our actions take care of themselves. This is a serious problem in the sports world in this day and time. There are so many "look at me" athletes that have to let everyone know how good they are on a daily basis. For example, the receiver who makes a great catch and then gets up and does a little dance as to say "did you see that? Look what I did." Too often he forgets the fact that simply stated in his job description as a receiver is to catch the ball. Too often we lose all humility when we feel we have accomplished something great, and we need to let everyone know about it, and we need to let them know loudly. The best players are the ones who keep their head down, do their job, and hear praise for their actions and not for their words. We should be humble in both word and deed, knowing that all we have is truly a gift from God, and it is to His glory that we should live.

What does it mean to be humble? Is it just making sure you thank the right people in a post-game press conference? Sadly, that is what I feel the word humility has come to mean to many people. I love hearing the Lord's name mentioned on T.V. by professional athletes, and I love that they thank God. However, too often it is those same people thanking God who play dirty and cuss loud enough for the first 15 rows of the stadium to hear. If they really wanted to give God the glory, they wouldn't do it as a cliché phrase in a post-game presser, but they would do it with their play on the field. A humble person shows his humility through his actions, not just his words. To me, being humble means being coachable and since I have gotten into coaching, I understand what that phrase means more than ever. Someone who is coachable is someone who is willing to take advice and always willing to learn. A coach can tell a player something until he is blue in the face (a phrase my dad used to describe how many times he had to tell me things when I was in little league), but if that player is not willing to make the adjustments, the coach is simply wasting his time. If a player is coachable, he doesn't have to use the phrase "I'm trying" because it can be seen in his actions. Take baseball for example. If I tell a player to hit the ball the other way, and he pulls the next five pitches and then says, "I'm trying," let me be the first one to break the news to you, he's not. You can tell if a player is trying by the adjustments he makes. If he hits the next five pitches foul the other way, then although he didn't put a ball in the field of play, you can see that he made the effort to do what he was told. I have come to the conclusion that there are two reasons people refuse to be coachable: 1: They already think they know the best way to do everything or 2: They just flat out do not care. The player who already thinks he knows everything is destined for failure because he refuses to practice, and although his talents may be great, he will never improve and will eventually fall into the extremely average category. The player who does not care is destined for the same fate because he refuses to push himself and have self-motivation to become better, and he also will eventually fall into the extremely average category IF he is not there already. We must always keep an open mind and be willing to learn and take advice from those who have been there and already had those experiences. The exact same principle applies to our Christian lives. Those Christians who already think they know all they need to know will never grow in Christ and will never get where they need to be spiritually. They refuse to listen to the advice of their elders who have perhaps been in the very same situation and seen how things turn out. The old saying goes, "If you're not getting better, you're getting worse." As Christians, if we are not growing in Christ then our faith will eventually die off. The Christian who does not care is one that is in serious trouble. Not only could he hurt himself, but he could hurt others around him as well. In sports, if you have a player who does not care, he is not going to help the team, and ultimately, all he will be doing is bringing it down. As a Christian, if you do not care then you will damage your own soul, and your actions can potentially bring other Christians down with you or possibly keep someone from ever coming to know Christ at all! Being humble means being coachable in all things at all times.

Lou Gehrig was one of the greatest baseball players of all time. He is a Hall of Famer and will be go down as a legend of the game forever. In his farewell speech on July 4, 1939, he showed us what it means to have humility even when you possess serious talent:

"Fans, for the past two weeks you have been reading about the bad break I got. Yet today I consider myself the luckiest man on the face of the earth. I have been in ballparks for seventeen years and have never received anything but kindness and encouragement from you fans.

Look at these grand men. Which of you wouldn't consider it the highlight of his career just to as-

sociate with them for even one day? Sure, I'm lucky. Who wouldn't consider it an honor to have known Jacob Ruppert? Also, the builder of baseball's greatest empire, Ed Barrow? To have spent six years with that wonderful little fellow, Miller Huggins? Then to have spent the next nine years with that outstanding leader, that smart student of psychology, the best manager in baseball today, Joe McCarthy? Sure, I'm lucky.

When the New York Giants, a team you would give your right arm to beat, and vice versa, sends you a gift — that's something. When everybody down to the groundskeepers and those boys in white coats remember you with trophies — that's something. When you have a wonderful mother-in-law who takes sides with you in squabbles with her own daughter — that's something. When you have a father and a mother who work all their lives so that you can have an education and build your body — it's a blessing. When you have a wife who has been a tower of strength and shown more courage than you dreamed existed — that's the finest I know.

So I close in saying that I might have been given a bad break, but I've got an awful lot to live for. Thank you."— Lou Gehrig at Yankee Stadium

What a site I'm sure it was to see a person who, at that time, had played in the most consecutive games in Major League Baseball and had earned the nickname the Iron Horse. He could have stood there and gone on and on about how he was a legend and how he should be remembered, but he didn't. He only thanked those around him that helped get him to where he was all the way down to the groundskeeper. This is a glimpse of what humility looks like.

We read in James 4:10, "Humble yourselves in the sight of the Lord, and He will lift you up." This could never be put more simply than it is here in the book of James. If we will only humble ourselves in all that we do here on this earth, we will be lifted up one day. We will receive a reward but not the one that so many look for as they walk this earth. The praise of men may escape us, but the true reward is the praise of our Father in heaven. We read in Luke chapter 18 about the story of the Publican and the Pharisee. Starting in verse 10, it says, *"Two men went up to the temple to pray, one a Pharisee and the other a tax collector. The Pharisee stood and prayed thus with himself, 'God, I thank You that I am not like other men – extortioners, unjust, adulterers, or even as this tax collector. I fast twice a week; I give tithes of all that I possess.' And the tax collector, standing afar off, would not so much as raise his eyes to heaven, but beat his breast, saying, 'God be merciful to me a sinner!' I tell you, this man went down to his house justified rather than the other; for everyone who exalts himself will be humbled, and he who humbles himself will be exalted."* Those who want to sit around and discuss all the wonderful things that they do will never have more than their own conversations while those that realize they still have room to grow will always have room to do so. We must always keep this in mind as a Christian people. When I was younger, I did not get an allowance for doing chores around the house. Much to my chagrin, my dad always told me that I should not get paid for doing the things that I was supposed to do anyway. Now, while this upset me then, it makes perfect sense now. The same goes in our spiritual lives. We should not expect praise for inviting people to worship service or having a Bible study with someone. If the reason we are doing those things is to receive praise of men then we are doing them all for the wrong reason, and just as the player who cusses and then thanks God, we are all talk and no walk. We should do those things because we want to, because we are commanded to do so in the word of God, and because we want to help share the good news of the gospel with those around us.

So, what can we take from the 6th inning? We must be humble in every aspect of our life. If we are humble, that means we are coachable and always willing and ready to learn and grow. If we are humble, we may not receive the instant gratification praise of men, but our reward will be much greater when we are exalted with our Father in heaven. Be coachable, be humble, and know that to God be the glory.

"The superior man is modest in his speech, but exceeds in his actions."
                                                    -Confucius

The 7th Inning

Trust In The Game Plan

"The most practical, beautiful, workable philosophy in the world won't work-if you won't."
-Zig Ziglar

The 7th inning is all about the ability to trust what is put before you and take on the task with all of your might. It is extremely hard to do something "all out" if you do not have trust in what you are doing. Think about a job or chore you had to do at some point in your life. You may not have given your best effort because you really didn't see the true point in what you were doing. The same can be said for the game of life. In order for us to give our maximum effort, we first have trust in the game plan and know that no matter the circumstances, things are going to work out.

Game plans have always been a part of sports. Football coaches watch film for hours on end in order to create the perfect game plan to beat a team. Baseball coaches go watch numerous games and talk to other coaches in order to get the perfect scouting report on a team so that they can create a plan for how they want to approach situations. Game plans have been and always will be one of the many secrets to any team's success. Think about when the star player is interviewed after the game. What does he say? "Coach put in a great game plan this week and we executed." Without the game plan, there would be nothing to execute which means there would be no success.

I saw the usefulness of game plans first hand when I was working with the baseball program at UNA. Now, I guess they are not really called "game plans" in baseball, but ultimately, that's what it is. Your team gets a scouting report on the other team, and you devise how you will approach a pitcher or hitter based off what you have in your report. You make a plan. The night before a weekend series during our team meeting, we would go over the game plan. The coaches would explain certain pitchers and their tendencies, and the pitchers and catchers would get a copy of the other team's hitters' scouting reports so they could devise a plan on how to pitch to them. That is how we developed our game plan, and I'll be honest, when everyone bought in to what we were trying to do, we were usually pretty successful. If we knew that the other team was weak at third base, we may want to lay down some bunts early and use our speed and test his arm. If we had a player who was red hot at the plate, we probably want to keep from throwing him a fastball down the heart of the plate. All of these concepts may seem simple, but they can make a dramatic difference between winning and losing a ball game. Now, the next key after trusting the game plan is executing the game plan. A team can have all the faith in the world that what they have mapped out will work, but if they cannot execute their plan then they are not going to see any success. Back when I was playing football in high school, we had an offensive coordinator that believed strongly in the power to execute a game plan. He told us that it didn't matter what down it was or what he called. If all 11 players on the field are doing their part to execute then it should work every time. He once said, "If we call a quarterback draw on 4th and 30 and all 11 guys believe in the play call and execute their job then it will score." At the time, we all laughed at this and thought it to be a bit silly, but looking back, he really did make a great point. For every play that a football team runs, everyone has some sort of assignment. Most of the time, every person on the defensive side of the ball is supposed to be accounted for by one of the offensive players. If every player did his job on any given play then why wouldn't it be a touchdown every time? It is silly to think about when we think of the ins and outs of the game and what all goes in to making a play call in today's world of sports, but it really is a simple principle. Know the game plan; trust the game plan; execute the game plan.

As Christians, if we simply replace the word "game" with "God" then we have a simple principle of living the right Christian life. We are to trust in God's game plan all the time because He has never nor will He ever make a mistake. He has a game plan mapped out, and if we will simply learn to understand His game plan the best we can, learn not to question his game plan, and learn to execute His game plan then we will find serious success when it comes to overcoming the world.

Trusting God's game plan is something that I feel many of us, as Christians, have a problem with on numerous occasions. We want to trust in His plan, but we get too worried and concerned that His plan is not going to match up with our plan, and then we lose all sight of whose plan we need to be following (everybody follow that?). Now, I'm not telling you to be the tumbleweed that blows in the wind with no direction saying, "I'm just waiting to figure out God's plan." That is not at all what I mean. Make plans, and set aside things you want to accomplish, but don't lose all hope when what you had planned does not fit exactly with what God has planned. I heard a preacher one time preach a sermon on the will of God. He told a story about how his wife was in the hospital while they were both still very young in their marriage. There was a serious issue that had to be addressed, and he was becoming legitimately concerned about the health of his young bride. While he sat in the waiting room praying, he asked God to watch over his wife and if it be His will to get her back to good health again. However, he mentioned in that sermon that what he prayed was not really what he meant, and he did not realize it till some time later. He said, "I said if it be His will, but what I was thinking and wanting was his will to be my will."

52

We do this quite often as Christians, I believe. We may say, "If it be Thy will" in our prayers, but ultimately, we want the Lord's will to be our will. We simply need to trust that His will is right whether or not it matches up with ours. As I mentioned earlier, God has never made a mistake, and if His will does not match up with ours, it is not because He hates us or because He does not want to give us what we want; it is simply because it was a part of His game plan, and we need to trust that it was right. The last thing we can possibly try to do is fully understand God and His ways. It says in Isaiah 55:8, "For My thoughts are not your thoughts, Nor are your ways My ways, says the Lord." We are simple humans here on this earth, and no matter how hard we try, we will never fully understand the way of our God. We just have to trust in Him and know that He does what He does with a purpose and with a plan for our lives. Romans 8:28 says, *"And we know that all things work together for good to those who love God, to those who are the called according to His purpose."*

When it comes to executing the Lord's game plan, it is all about doing as we are commanded in His word. That does not mean picking and choosing the parts of His word that we like and just applying them to our lives, but it means using the whole word and making it the model by which we live our lives. We are blessed because we have numerous examples of those who trusted and executed God's game plan. In fact, another book could probably be written about the numerous people in scripture who put their faith and trust in what the Lord had set out for them. Of course, the greatest of all is God's son, Jesus. He came down to earth to live as a human like you and me as a part of God's game plan. He was tempted just as we are, and He was mocked and ridiculed. Yet, He did it all executing God's game plan. He gave his own life on the cross for all of mankind because He trusted in God's game plan and He executed it with maximum effort. As a man, He lived a perfect life because of the execution of the game plan that was set before Him. What an example to live by.

What can we take from the 7th inning? We have to fully trust in God's game plan that is set before us. We will not always understand it, and it is not our job to do so, but it is our job to trust in the plan and execute it to the best of our ability. Without a complete trust in the game plan that is set before us, there is no way that we can fully overcome the world. With trust and execution in God's game plan, we can know that we will be winners when our game of life is done. Proverbs 3:5-6, *"Trust in the Lord with all your heart, and lean not on your own understanding; In all yours ways acknowledge Him, and He shall direct your paths."*

"Things turn out best for people who make the best of the way things turn out."

-Art Linkletter

The 7th Inning
Stretch

As we hit the 7th inning stretch, we can look back on the past 7 innings and see what we have learned. We know that we cannot have one inning without the other, as they all make up the sum of the victory and not just one inning alone. We must first be willing to set our goals of what we wish to accomplish as Christians here on this earth. Again, I strongly recommend that you write down these goals so that you can refer back to them regularly. Make long-term and short-term goals, and find ways to daily remind yourself of the goals that you have set in place. Once you have made your goals, it is then time to prioritize your life in a way that will allow you to achieve these goals. If you do not get your priorities in line then your goals will never be met. Next, we have to practice and study to always grow and learn more. There is always more to learn, and there is always room to grow. As long as we are willing to continue to work to get better, we can overcome some of the shortcomings that we may face. Then, we must be willing to surround ourselves with winners. That may mean letting go of the people and things that will only bring us down and keep us from reaching the goals that we set out to accomplish in the 1st inning. Surrounding ourselves with winners is the best way to keep us strong in Christ and keep us moving forward. We must also know our roles and talents and carry them out with maximum effort. Never think one role is bigger than the other because all roles hold equal importance. Every person can do something to further their own Christian lives and help reach out to others about Christ as well. If you feel that you have the talents to take on more roles, then do so. Never be satisfied with where you are if you know you can do better or if you know you can do more. We must then push ourselves to be all that we can be. Life is not a spectator sport, and those who don't push themselves will never improve to be where they need to be and go where they need to go. In all these things, we must remain humble. It is all to God's glory that we are where we are and do what we do. We are never to have the "look at me attitude" because praise from men here on this earth is nothing in comparison to the praise that we will receive from our Father in heaven. Finally, we must trust in the God's game plan. We don't have to understand it all the time, but we must be willing to do whatever it takes to execute to the best of our ability. He has a plan set out for us, and if we will execute it then the reward will be oh so great.

We have now gone through the first 7 innings, and there are only two more to go. They carry just as much importance as the previous 7, and our ultimate goal of overcoming the world cannot be met unless we push full steam ahead and finish the game on the Lord's team. The last two innings are vital to our success just as the first 7 were. Not because I say so but because that is what God has laid out in his word. In the last two innings, we will talk about playing with a purpose and persevering during difficult times. Both are vital to winning in any athletic competition but even more so in the game that really matters - the game of life. Here is a little something to prepare ourselves for what is ahead in the last two innings:

OUR PURPOSE

What is our purpose
In this life we live,
And before it is all over
Will we give all we have to give?

Will we make every second count
And breathe each breathe like our last?
Will we live in the present
And leave all other things in the past?

Will we work to live like He did
And follow His footprints in the sand?
When people want to test our faith
Will we take a Holy stand?

Will we always remember
That though we may do wrong,
He stays ready to forgive us
And once again make us strong?

Will we work to share the truth
Of His Holy word?
Will we tell it far and wide?
The greatest story ever heard.

Will we live our life to please Him
For that's really why we're here?
It is our purpose in this life
To always keep Him near.

-Ben Stevenson

The 8th Inning

Play With A Purpose

"A ship is safe in harbor, but that's not what ships are for."
-William Shedd

Anything that has ever been worth doing in life has always had a purpose. Whether it is sports, business, or our everyday activities, there is a purpose to what we do. It is up to us to discover that purpose and decide whether or not the purpose is worth the work. This is extremely vital in our Christian lives as our overall purpose is to get to heaven, and we have to always remember to live our lives with that purpose in mind. When we lose sight of our purpose, we lose sight of everything worth fighting for in this life.

In sports, the purpose of any athletic event is clearly to win. Anybody who was ever any good in athletics was someone who set out to win all the time. In Major League Baseball, a team plays 162 regular season games. Now, to my knowledge, I do not know of any team that has ever gone 162-0. Baseball is a game full of many ups and downs and highs and lows and a player, or team, can get on a cold streak just as easily and quickly as they can get on a hot streak. I have not run the numbers, but I would imagine that the chance of a MLB team going 162-0 would be extremely, extremely slim. Yet, if a reporter were to go to a player during spring training and ask him if he wanted to win every game that year, I can bet the player would say YES. Knowing that the chances are small, he would still love to win 162 games and be completely undefeated. To take it a step further, I would venture to say that he would like to win every at-bat during the season as well. Keep in mind baseball is a game where the best hitters of all time have failed 7 out of 10 times. Yet, I can all but promise that said player would love to win every single at-bat when he stepped into the box that year. To take things a step further, I bet that he would also love to win every single pitch that year as well. To never get tied-up or thrown off. To never swing at junk out of the strike zone or watch a called third strike. Now, we are talking about something that is even more impossible than the first two scenarios. Yet, if asked, I am sure a player would love to win every single pitch he saw that year. You may be telling yourself, "That is silly. These are impossible scenarios and any player who considered himself a realist would know that these things could just not happen." Well, you would be right. Not only is a team probably never going to win every game they play during a baseball season, but a player is not going to win every at-bat, much less every pitch that he sees. However, that does not keep that player and his team from striving to do that very thing. A team takes the field every day to win the ball game. A player steps into the box to win the at-bat, and he readies himself to win every pitch. Just because these goals are near, if not totally, impossible, that does not keep him from striving for them. He continues to strive for that perfection although it is almost always out of his reach. Robert Browning once wrote, "Ah, but a man's reach should exceed his grasp, or what's heaven for?" Just as a player strives for these unreachable goals in a ball game, we, as Christians, should make it our purpose in life to strive for the perfect life that Christ left as an example for us. Is perfection a realistic goal here on earth? No. There has been one perfect man, and it was Christ. Romans 3:23 says, "For all have sinned and fall short of the glory of God." Often this verse is used as a scapegoat for the mistakes and slip ups of Christian people. "Well, I'm not perfect," they will sometimes say or, "I'm only human." Are we not perfect because we openly choose not to be, or are we not perfect because we are human and at times the devil can get the best of us? Our number one purpose in this life should be to get to heaven, but I don't think that we should be trying to do as little as we have to do just to make it in. I honestly feel that we should be striving for perfection and to be Christ like every day. Our purpose is to get to heaven, yes, but it is also to take others with us and show them how a Christian is supposed to be and act through the life that we live. We have to understand our purpose and understand that there is no greater purpose in the entire world than that of serving God and letting his light shine through us.

There is no doubt that a large part of our purpose here on this earth is to spread the good news of the Gospel and to bring others to know Christ. Another purpose we have as Christians is to help make sure that our brothers and sisters in Christ stay the course with us. We talked back in inning 5 about pushing ourselves to do what is necessary. The same could be said when it comes to our brothers and sisters in Christ. We have to be willing to push each other in order to reach our goals together. Often times I feel that we are afraid to do this as Christians because we are afraid of hurting the other's feelings or coming off as a "know it all." Of course, there is a right way and a wrong way to push someone, but it is something that needs to be done. This reminds me of that team that has great chemistry but no team leadership. Everyone on the team gets along extremely well, and the team chemistry is there without a doubt, but when the going gets tough and someone needs to step up, everyone is afraid to call out another teammate because they are friends, and they don't want to make them mad or upset them. I have seen this more than once in my short time in athletics, and it is odd to see when everyone is too good of friends to simply tell someone, "You need to step up." We cannot be this way in our Christian lives. Again, there is definitely a right way and a wrong way to approach a fellow Christian, but we have to be willing to hold one another accountable in the way we live our lives. When a player calls out the other, it does not mean that he has made every play and hit every ball so he now has the right to call someone out. He has made his share of mistakes as well, but he knows his teammate can do a whole lot better than he is doing. The same goes with our Christian brothers and sisters. When we approach someone, it does not mean that we are perfect or never make mistakes. It simply means that as a loving Christian, we want to see that person succeed, and we know they are not living up to who they are and what they know. Holding one another accountable is something that I think can go a long way in the church today. If we are all striving for perfection and reaching for the same goal of heaven then this should be an easy task.

Finally, we must play the game of life with the purpose of worship. Too often in today's modern world, we have grown tired of going to worship services. We will hear so many people say, "God knows my heart, so it doesn't matter if I'm in church or not." They are correct in stating that God knows their heart. This is true, but if your heart is really where it needs to be then why in the world would you not want to go worship God with fellow Christians! We are to praise God in all the things that we do (remember the inning about humility), and we are to worship Him when the saints are called together for worship services and on our own. To fully understand the importance or worship, we have to understand heaven. When I attended the Lone Cedar Church of Christ, we had many youth devotionals down in the basement of the annex building. These were always very uplifting, and the things that I liked most about these devos was the fact that we would turn off all the lights in the room and just sing for hours. It was a beautiful thing, and I could really feel the presence of Christ there with us more than ever. My good friend Eddie Matthews (the youth minister there at the time) often told us, "If you don't like singing, you won't like heaven." This always stuck with me, and it is something that I have thought back on many times. I, along with I'm sure many others, have pictured heaven as a big vacation where we get rewarded and just get to relax and enjoy ourselves. That really is not heaven at all. Heaven is a place where we will be worshipping God all the time. It is not an eternity of "free time" or "me time," but it is an eternity of worship. If we do not enjoy going to worship services here on this earth, how can we ever expect to enjoy a heaven where we worship all the time? Our purpose here on this earth is to worship God and be excited about doing so. This should never be a burden or a chore, but it should be a privilege that we never take for granted.

In Hebrews 12:1-2 we read, *"Therefore we also, since we are surrounded by so great a cloud of witnesses, let us lay aside every weight, and the sin which so easily ensnares us, and let us run with endurance the race that is set before us, looking unto Jesus, the author and finisher of our faith, who for the joy that was set before Him endured the cross, despising the shame, and has set down at the right hand of the throne of*

God." This should be our purpose in the life that we live here on this earth. It is to run and finish the race that is set before us as Christians and always keep our eyes on the finish line - Heaven. 1 Corinthians 9:24-27 says, *"Do you not know that those who run in a race run all, but one receives the prize? Run in such a way that you may obtain it. And everyone who competes for the prize is temperate in all things. Now they do it to obtain a perishable crown, but we an imperishable crown. Therefore I run thus: not with uncertainly. Thus I fight: not as one who beats the air. But I discipline my body and bring it into subjection, lest, when I have preached to others, I myself should become disqualified."* We run such a race in this game of life not for the rewards of men and not for anything that we can or will receive here on this earth but for an incorruptible crown of a home in heaven. We may love many things here on this earth. I have already made mention of my love for my family and for athletics. There are few things I love more in this world than those two things. However, in the grand scheme of it all, the only things that matter are not things of this earth. They are things that I will receive one day when my life here on this earth is over. When my game clock strikes zero and I take my final breath, I want to have lived a life where my purpose and my goal was for things above. I hope and pray that you feel the same way.

So, what all can we take from the 8th inning? We must know and always keep in mind that we have to live this life with a heavenly purpose. We need to strive for perfection. It may be out of our reach, but if Jesus set the bar, why not try our best to be as close to that bar as possible. We have to live with the purpose of spreading the good news of the Gospel and always working to help and push ourselves and those around us to do that very same thing. It is a much easier race to run when you have a support team with you at all times. Finally, we must live with the purpose to worship. We should want to praise God in all that we do, and we should be excited about the opportunity to worship Him at any time but especially when we can all gather together and worship as Christians. There may be many things that we love while here on this earth, but none should be more important than our heavenly purpose while we are here. If we can live every day with a purpose and goal of heaven in mind then we can truly over-come and win the game of life.

"If nothing worthwhile exists under the sun, our only hope must live above it."

-John Maxwell

The 9th Inning

Persevere

"Victory belongs to the most persevering."
-Napoleon Bonaparte

We have finally reached the 9th inning in this game of life, and I can think of only one thing that is left for us to do. If we have made it through the first 8 innings, we have set our goals/priorities, practiced/studied, surrounded ourselves with winners, understood our role, pushed ourselves, stayed humble, trusted in the game plan, and played with a purpose. Now, all that is left to do is persevere. This is the final step to overcoming the world, and it is not easy task. All the breaks are not going to go our way, and there will be times when it seems that nothing can go right, but we have to press on and know that *"If God is for us, who can be against us?"* –Romans 8:31. There will be times when we will have to rely on others for help and when we will have to trust in the game plan more than ever before, but we must always keep in mind that the reward of heaven is worth every hardship and struggle that we could possibly face. Heaven is what makes living here on this earth meaningful, and it should be the finish line that is ever on our minds in moments of struggle.

Anybody who has ever played any type of sport before knows that the breaks never always go your way. There are times when you feel that you have done everything right, but your results are just not there. This can be extremely frustrating to an athlete that knows he has put in all the hard work necessary for success. Baseball is a game where this can be seen more than any other. It is such an up and down game that a player can be absolutely smoking the ball and hitting it right at people, but on the other side of the coin, another player could be getting little dinker hits that barely drop in over the infield. Now, the first player mentioned is obviously seeing the ball better and making better contact. He is just not having any luck; he is catching all the bad breaks. Over time, however, that first player is usually going to have a much more successful career because the other player's luck of getting dink hits (or dying quails as they are sometimes called) will eventually run out, and he is not making solid enough contact to overcome the breaks when his luck does run out. This is just a simple example of the ups and downs of baseball.

Sometimes no matter how many hours you spend in the batting cages or taking ground balls, you are going to hit a ball right at someone or the ball is going to take a funny hop, and you are going to catch a bad break. This is just simply the frustrating, annoying, tiresome nature of the game. I mentioned in the 8th inning about how a team in the majors has never won 162 games in a season. Now, they may have been extremely prepared for the season and had all the talent in the world, but at least a handful of times, they are going to find themselves with a loss simply because the breaks didn't go their way. The great teams are the ones that can overcome this and come back out the next day ready to start fresh and new and put a new winning streak together. The unsuccessful teams are the ones who can never overcome their deficient and simply become accustomed to losing. We must be willing to overcome the "bad breaks" that we sometimes get dealt and push forward to another day where we are ready to show our strengths.

As Christians, we must keep this same concept in mind as we go through our daily lives. The game of life is without question a game full of ups and downs. There are times when we will be on top of the world and others where we feel like there is nothing we can do right. The only way to get through these low points is to persevere. The definition of the word persevere is to persist in anything undertaken; maintain a purpose in spite of difficulty, obstacles, or discouragement; continue steadfastly. In my short life here on this earth, I can know without a shadow of a doubt that you and I are going to face all of those things during our lives. This is even more so the case for the Christian people. I have said it before, and I will say it again - We are living in the devil's world. Life here on this earth would be and will be much easier if we just gave in and "had some fun" while we were here. If we just threw the Bible out the window and took life as it came, I suppose there could probably be fewer hardships during our life time. Sadly, this is how some people think. They live so much in the here and now that they have not given their eternal life one single thought. While they are living the life in the devil's world, their eternal life map is being written slowly but surely for a place that I know no man truly wants to go.

As Christians, we have to understand that life here on this earth is simply to prepare us for what is to come. Any hardships we may face here will be erased tenfold once we enter through the gates of heaven. We will not give our life here on earth a second thought, and we will know that everything was worth the prize. We are going to catch bad breaks at times. There will be times where we fall into a pit and need the help of God and our teammates to help get us out. There will be times when we may continue to study the scripture with a person, and they just want nothing to do with changing their lives to live the right Christian life. There will be times when we will be deemed uncool, Bible huggers, too religious, too uptight, no fun, and called hypocrites simply because we go to church even though they have no clue how we live our lives. These can be trying times for any person. It is hard sometimes to take failure or ridicule on an almost daily basis when it would be easier to simply give in and let the world win, but we have to persevere.

I would be remiss if I wrote a book about sports, especially baseball, without mentioning my all-time favorite baseball player. I have liked many players over the years, but there has always been one that stood out among the rest for me and that is the "Iron Man," Cal Ripken Jr. I have always loved everything about how Ripken played the game of baseball. This was a man who played on losing teams and winning teams, played two different positions, played without the flash and "look at me" attitude that so many players have today, and while doing all that played in 2,632 consecutive games. He played in every game from 1982 until 1998 and had an incredible career in between. I have had the opportunity to read one of Cal's books, Get in the Game, and it truly is amazing all the things that Ripken was able to overcome in his illustrious career. Considering that few players make it through a season of 162 games without an injury or an off day, it is amazing to think that Cal played 16 seasons without missing a day of work. He had to play through numerous injuries and games where it seemed that he could do nothing right, and yet, he continued to press on and go to work day in and day out.

As Christians, we have to have the same mindset of perseverance in our Christian works. In everything we do, we must have a "never quit" attitude. The words "NEVER QUIT" are words that almost every athlete that has ever played a sport has heard. They are often used at motivational speaking engagements and posted all over weight room and training room walls. Having the ability to persevere for one more round, one more quarter, or one more inning when your body feels like it has nothing else to give is what separates the good players from the great players. It is what wins championships and creates dynasties. However, this never quit, persevering attitude has to be taken beyond the playing field. The people who take this attitude with them in every endeavor in their lives are the people that are truly successful. We, as a Christian people, must take this attitude with us in our everyday Christian walk. The Bible talks about this never quit attitude in 1 Thessalonians 1:3, *"Remembering without ceasing your work of faith, labor of love, and patience of hope in our Lord Jesus Christ in the sight of God our Father."* We read in 2 Timothy about how Paul has fought the good fight and finished his course and how he looks forward to his reward of heaven, and we read in 2 Timothy 2:3 how we are to *"endure hardship as a good soldier of Jesus Christ."* These are just a few of the examples of perseverance laid out in God's word.

Obviously, one of the greatest stories of perseverance is found in the book of Job. We read in Job 13:15, "Though he slay me, yet will I trust in Him. Even so, I will defend my own ways before Him." Here Job is willing to say that no matter what he is put through, even to his own death, he will continue to trust in the Lord. What a true concept of the never quit, persevering attitude! We must be willing to take on this same attitude in our Christian lives. We have done all of the preparation. Now we must never quit; we must preserve.

So, what can be taken from the 9th inning? We must be willing to persevere through any obstacle that is set before us. We can overcome anything if we are willing to persevere through the hardships that we face. It is almost comical to think of the struggles we have in this life compared to those written about in the Bible. If they can overcome and keep their faith in God, there is no reason why we should not be able to do the same. Ephesians 6:13 says, "Therefore take up the whole armor of God, that you may able to withstand in the evil day, and having done all, to stand." That has to be our mindset when it comes to our Christian perseverance. Having done all the preparation and work to overcome the world we now have to stand, never quit, push forward, and persevere.

"Patience and perseverance has a magical effect before which difficulties disappear and obstacles vanish."

-John Quincy Adams

Extra Innings

A Game Recap

We have spent the last 9 innings talking about 9 different ways to overcome the world and how each of these steps is vital to our overall success as Christians while living in the devil's world. Again, I reiterate the fact that this not a new idea that I came up with all on my own. These things are laid out in the Bible, and all I did was make them into a process. God has given us all we need to be successful in our Christian lives and we must be willing to take the advice and resources given to us and use them to further our cause as Christians. Here in the extra innings, I just want to close out all of what was covered in innings 1-9 and remind you that even when we have won the first 9 innings in our Christian lives, the game is not over.

In baseball, extra innings is the time where many separate the winners from the losers. A person can play great for 9 innings, but if he does not have the drive and will to finish then he has wasted his own time and the time of his teammates. Think of the extra inning ball games that you have seen in your lifetime. When they are finally won with that walk-off hit or walk-off homerun, the crowd and the team erupt with excitement and cheer. Why? Because all of the hard work and effort that was put forth the entire game has finally produced the end result that was worked for. The longest professional baseball game ever played was between the Pawtucket Red Sox and the Rochester Red Wings. These teams were two minor league affiliates of the Boston Red Sox and Baltimore Orioles, and the afore-mentioned Cal Ripken Jr. played in this very game. This game lasted 33 innings over the course of eight hours and twenty-five minutes. The game started on April 18th and went well into the morning of the 19th. After 8 hours of play, at 4:07 after the 32nd inning, the game was stopped. Instead of resuming it on the next day because of risk of injury with a double header, the game resumed the next time the Red Wings came in town on June 23rd. This is by far the greatest example I can think of where two teams simply were not willing to give in and let the other team win. What a battle! We have to have that type of attitude throughout our Christian lives. There is a reason that the 9th inning is about perseverance, and that is because if we can master that concept in the 9th inning then it is much easier for us to take it with us into extra innings. We have to have the mindset of not letting our opponent, the devil, get the best of us and take the lead in our game of life. When the going gets tough, we have to put on more steam. I feel that the extra innings will be much easier to conquer if we have done our part in innings 1-9. If we have set our goals and prioritized our life to meet those goals then we have something to strive for. If we are willing to practice and study to get better then we will know that we have worked hard and put ourselves in a situation to succeed. If we surround ourselves with winners then we will have a good foundation on which we can rely for support during struggling times. If we know our role and talents then we will be able to execute what needs to be done successfully. If we push ourselves then we will know that we have worked way too hard and come way too far to give in now. As long as we stay humble, we will always be reminded that it is God who has allowed us to be who we are and where we are, and it is to Him that the glory should be given. If we trust in the game plan then we will realize that even though we may not understand it all of the time, we will continue to trust in Him because His ways are greater than our ways. If we play with a purpose then we are playing with an attitude of the end result in mind. Finally, if we can persevere then we will know that even when hard times come, we can and will overcome what is before us. If we can truly conquer all of these things in the first 9 innings then it really does make the extra innings in life that much easier. It allows us to complete our game of life on the winning team.

Let's look at a few passages in the Bible that remind us of how a Christian should be. In Galatians 2:20, we read, *"I have been crucified with Christ; it is no longer I who live, but Christ lives in me; and the life which I now live in the flesh I live by faith in the Son of God, who loved me and gave Himself for me."* I think there is a lot of power in that statement "the life which I now live." This shows a complete change of life and attitude after becoming a Christian. We now are to live a life that is completely devoted to the Son of God who gave Himself for us. I look in Job 1:8 and it says, "Then the Lord said to Satan, 'Have you considered My servant Job, that there is none like him on the earth, a blameless and upright man, one who fears God and shuns evil?" I honestly feel that it should be our goal as Christians here on this earth to be described by God in this manner. To live a life where God can look down at us and say these types of things about us and how we live our lives and how we affect other people's lives as well. What an incredible honor to be talked about in this way by the Lord!

There is no doubt that we, as Christians, have the ability to overcome the world as talked about in 1 John 5:4. We have the ability through God, but we have to be willing to put in the work to obtain our goals. It goes without saying that it will not be an easy journey. Things will be difficult, and there will be times when we may feel that there truly is no way we can win the game, but we have to remember who is in control and trust in Him. We have an abundance of choices in this world in which we live. The choice of eternity leaves us with two options. Something to keep in mind - If earth was the place to be, Jesus would have stayed. Your true home can be hot or holy. Thank God it's your choice. Stay strong, and overcome.

Winning the Game of Life

Winning in the game of life
Is something we must do,
If we want to be with our lord
When this game is through.

Winning isn't everything
Is what they sometimes say,
But really winning is what matters
In this game we play.

Winning on this earth
Gets you recognition from man,
But being a winner for the Lord
Is something that few people understand.

It doesn't get you a trophy, medal, or ring
It gives the prize of heaven
Which is out of them all, the greatest thing.

So how do we win
This spiritual game?
We look at what Christ did
And try to do the same.

The game is very hard
You don't have an easy road ahead.
But when you mess up, simply look to Christ
For that's why His blood was shed.

So when your game clock strikes zero
And your life on earth is done
Can you look at God on that day
And say, "The game of life I've won."?

-Ben Stevenson

To the Reader:

I thank you for taking the time to read my book. I hope that you have been able to take something from it that you can apply to your daily life. It was a joy to write for me as athletics and faith are very important in my life. I have always loved the connection between sports and faith by great New Testament men such as Paul and writing a book of this kind has always been a dream of mine. If this book was one of your first encounters with some of the scriptures used throughout and you would like to learn more scan the QR code below. It will take you to the Apologetics Press website that I have personally found as a great resource where there are Bible answers to Bible questions. Again, I thank you for taking the time to read my book and I hope it has been a blessing to you in your life. God Bless.

    -Ben